LOST IN SPACE

THE FLIGHT OF APOLLO 13

BY GARY BUSH
ILLUSTRATED BY NICK DERINGTON

STONE ARCH BOOKS
MINNEAPOLIS   SAN DIEGO

Graphic Flash is published by Stone Arch Books
151 Good Counsel Drive, P.O. Box 669
Mankato, Minnesota 56002
www.stonearchbooks.com

Library of Congress Cataloging-in-Publication Data
Bush, Gary R., 1942–
    Lost in Space: The flight of Apollo 13 / by Gary Bush; illustrated by Nick
Derington.
    p. cm. — (Graphic Flash)
    ISBN 978-1-4342-1162-0 (library binding)
    ISBN 978-1-4342-1378-5 (pbk.)
    1. Apollo 13 (Spacecraft)—Juvenile fiction. [1. Apollo 13 (Spacecraft)—
Fiction. 2. Mexcian Americans—Fiction.] I. Derington, Nick, ill. II. Title.
PZ7.B9646Lo 2009
[Fic]—dc22   2008032069

Summary: When 15-year-old Ramón Garza's grades start to slip, he's forced
to help out his mother after school. She's a food service worker at the NASA,
which is about to launch another rocket ship to the Moon. While there,
Ramon meets the crew and watches as *Apollo 13* soars into space on April
11, 1970. But only two days after the launch, the mission goes horribly wrong.

Creative Director: Heather Kindseth
Designer: Bob Lentz

1 2 3 4 5 6 14 13 12 11 10 09

Printed in the United States of America

TABLE OF CONTENTS

INTRODUCING...

Ken Mattingly

Gene Kranz

Maria Garza

Ramón Garza

-4-

CHAPTER 1

THE FIGHT

Later that day, my mother and I sat in Principal Morgan's office. "Mrs. Garza, this is the third time Ramón has been caught fighting in the last two months," he said.

"And his grades are dropping," my teacher, Mr. Morales, added. "He use to be an A and B student. Now if he gets a C, it's a miracle!"

"It's been a rough time for Ramón," said my mother. "And for me. My husband was killed in Vietnam last year."

I just sat there silently.

"I have received permission to have Ramón come to my work after school," she continued. "I'll make sure his grades and attitude improve."

My mother, Maria, worked for NASA at the Johnson Space Center. She wasn't an engineer, or a scientist, or an astronaut. She was a food service worker and ran the cafeteria where the engineers, scientists, and astronauts came to eat. That, I thought, was a nothing job.

She was serious. So every day I took the bus to the Johnson Space Center to do my homework and to work. It was a nothing job. I had to take food orders from people with real jobs and help clean the cafeteria. I hated working at the Space Center. I was sure everyone thought I was there because I was a troublemaker.

But people smiled and pronounced my name correctly. After a while, I began to take interest in my work. I even started to take an interest in the space program.

One January afternoon, I was sitting in my mother's cafeteria and having difficulty with a math problem. I asked my mother, "Can you help me with this long division?"

"When I'm finished with my work, Ramón," she answered.

"Maybe I can help," came a man's voice.

I looked up to see the face of Captain Jim Lovell. He was an astronaut who had been on several *Gemini* missions, the command module pilot on *Apollo 8*, and now commander of *Apollo 13*. Soon, he would walk on the Moon!

"Now let's see," he said. He sat down next to me and looked at the problem. "One hundred and fifty-six divided by 12. How many times does 12 go into 15, Ramón?"

"Once," I replied, feeling kind of stupid. I wished I didn't need the help.

"Mark it down," he said. "Now subtract 12 from 15, and you come up with what?"

"Three," I said.

"Okay," Lovell continued. "Bring down the 6 and you have?"

"Thirty-six," I said, exitedly. "Divide that by 12 and I have 13!"

"You know, Ramón," he said. "It's not impossible to be a Marine and an astronaut at the same time. John Glenn was a Marine. My crewmate Fred Haise served with the Marines too. Walt Cunningham, Vance Brand, and Cliff Williams are all Marines and astronauts."

"I'll bet it's hard," I said.

"Well, you have to go to college and study math, science, and aeronautics," Lovell said. "You have to learn how to fly and operate a jet."

"Flying a jet would be cool," I said.

Lovell smiled. "Yup, but NASA needs doctors, teachers, and scientists in the space program as well. It all requires study and, above all, bravery."

Bravery. My dad was brave, but he never got the chance to go to college. I would. I would become a Marine flyer and an astronaut. I'd show those kids at school.

After that, Captain Lovell must have spoken to the crew of *Apollo 13*. In the weeks that followed, he or Fred Haise or Ken Mattingly would stop by and help me with my math or science.

One day in March, Eugene Kranz, the flight director, came with them. It was amazing to have these men sitting at the table, helping me with my homework. "Your mother tells me tomorrow's your fifteenth birthday. How would you like a private tour of Mission Control?"

I couldn't contain my excitement. "Yes!"

That night, I couldn't sleep. I gazed out the window at the Moon. It seemed so bright and close. Commander Lovell had told me that the Moon was more than 200,000 miles from Earth. It would take *Apollo 13* five days to get there.

"Ramón, turn off the light," my mother called. "Tomorrow's a big day."

I awoke the next morning, glared at the clock, and wolfed down my breakfast. Ken Mattingly had volunteered to pick me up in ten minutes.

Ken had a great sports car, and we sped to the Manned Spacecraft Center. "I'll bet you're anxious to pilot the command module," I said.

"I sure am," Ken replied. "I've been training for a long time. I was lucky to be chosen for the space program."

It was more than luck. To be chosen, an astronaut had to be one of the top pilots.

At Mission Control, even for a Saturday, there was lots of activity. Technicians were checking their computers. In a few weeks, *Apollo 13* would launch for the Moon. Gene Kranz's station as flight director was near the top of the Center. Behind him was a glassed-in viewing area for VIPs, astronauts' families, and NASA officials.

Just then, a man came into the huge room.
Mr. Kranz called him over and then introduced
me. "Ramón, this is Jack Swigert," he said. "Jack
is Ken Mattingly's backup on *Apollo 13*."

We shook hands. "Your mother's Maria Garza,
right?" Swigert said. "She is a great woman, you
should be proud."

A great woman? I never thought of her that
way. She worked in the cafeteria. But maybe
her job was important. After all, it was NASA's
cafeteria. Everyone here was part of an historic
project.

"Jack," Mr. Kranz said. "Why don't you take
Ramón to see the capsule simulators?"

We drove over in Mr. Swigert's car, and he told
me how he became an astronaut. The more I
heard from the astronauts, the more I understood
how hard it would be to become one of them.

At the capsule simulator . . .
Crawl in the command capsule.
Really?!
There sure are a lot of controls.
There are indeed. Forty percent of our training is learning how to use the spacecraft navigation systems.
I could never learn all these buttons.
Sure you can, kid. It just takes time, and a little practice.

CHAPTER 2

THE MISSION BEGINS

April was a busy month for the *Apollo 13* crew. Eventually, they left for Cape Kennedy in Florida, which is now called Cape Canaveral. The huge Saturn 5 rocket was there, waiting to send the astronauts into space.

I missed their help with my homework. But to tell the truth, I was doing pretty well on my own.

Sometimes, I'd take box lunches up to Mission Control and watch the preparations from behind the glass of the VIP room. I really didn't understand it all, but I caught the excitement going on in front of me.

A few days before the launch, Ken Mattingly received some bad news. He'd been exposed to the German measles. Rather than taking a chance that he would get sick in space, NASA replaced him with his backup, Jack Swigert, as command capsule pilot.

Ken felt terrible. Captain Lovell argued with the doctors and told them that the measles weren't that serious. Lovell said that if Ken came down with them, he and Fred Haise could bring the spacecraft home. The doctors, however, weren't going to take any risks.

I was in the cafeteria when Ken and Mr. Kranz walked in. "Hi, Mr. Kranz. Hi, Ken. I'm sorry about you being replaced," I said softly.

Ken patted my shoulder. "Thanks, kid. There will be other spaceflights." But I could tell he was disappointed. Then Mr. Kranz stared at me.

"Wow! May I, Mom?" I asked.

She smiled. "Yes, if you promise to stay out of the way," she said.

"I promise!" I exclaimed.

Saturday, April 11, 1970, I was up at dawn, checking my model of the Saturn 5 rocket and the three parts of the *Apollo* spacecraft. First, there was *Odyssey*, the command module where the crew would spend most their time on the flight. Second, the service module, which contained the oxygen, water, and power. Finally, there was *Aquarius*, the lunar module, which would take Lovell and Haise to the surface of the Moon.

I took the bus to the Johnson Space Center and arrived at ten that morning. Only a few people were in the VIP room — the real action was in the main room called Mission Control. A package arrived for Gene Kranz. It was a white vest with the *Apollo* logo on it. Mr. Kranz always wore a vest during a launch. The men in the Control Center began to applaud, and I heard a few whistles.

Gene Kranz began to call out to the stations. "Boosters. Retro. Guidance. Surgeon," he said.

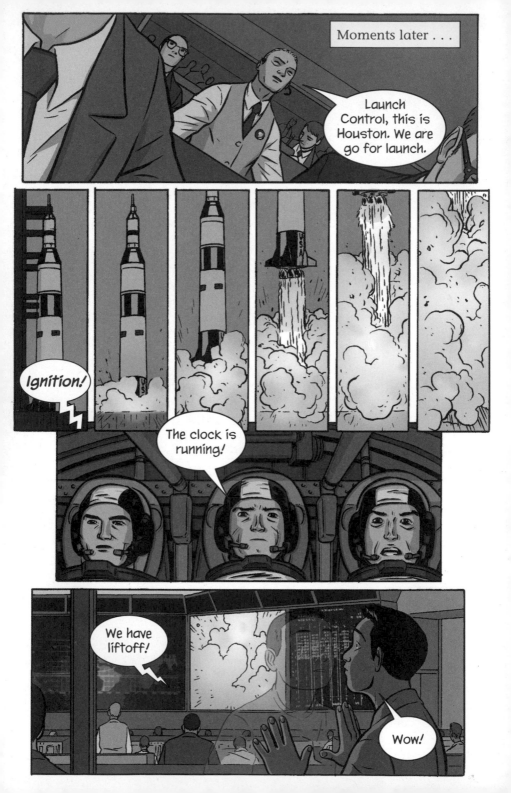

"Houston, we have cleared the tower at 13:13," someone called over the loudspeaker.

"Okay, guys we got it," Kranz answered.

Then, I heard Jim Lovell over the astronaut's speaker called the squawk box. "Houston, we've got a center engine cutoff."

"We're still go," the flight officer said. "We'll be all right as long as we don't lose another one."

"The other engines are good, so we're going to burn them for a little bit longer," the capsule communication officer told the crew.

I was worried about all of the commotion. But one of the engineers was sitting next to me. "It's routine from here on, kid," he said. "No worries."

The situation might have been routine for him, but it sure wasn't for me. This was the most exciting thing I had ever seen. These men were on the way to the Moon.

Before the crew could travel to the Moon, they had to pick up the LM, or lunar module. It was stored in the third stage of the Saturn rocket. That was Jack Swigert's job.

First, Jack had to separate the command module, or CM, from the third stage. That went very smoothly. Then, he had to line up on the LM. This was a tricky operation, but Jack was an excellent pilot.

From the squawk box, I heard Fred Haise call out the distance as Jack lined up. "Forty feet, twenty, ten, capture!" he exclaimed.

"Houston, we have hard dock," said Jack.

"Roger," replied Mission Control.

Fred's voice called out, "Okay, Houston, we have LM extraction."

"Like I said, Ramón, routine," the engineer said. He smiled and left the room.

I sat there for a long time watching and listening to the action. I'm not sure how late it was, but there was a shift change in Mission Control. Then I felt a tap on my shoulder.

The next day after church, I went to my room and turned on my NASA squawk box. Ken Mattingly had installed the radio in our house.

What I heard was mostly course corrections, and what I thought at the time was busywork. I hadn't realized then that all the things the crew had to do were needed to keep the spacecraft flying.

School the next day dragged by. The crew was going to broadcast that evening from space, and I wanted to watch it. When I got to NASA, I heard someone say, "The TV networks aren't going to broadcast the crew."

"Mom," I called to her. "Can we stay and watch them?"

"Did you finish your homework?" she asked.

"Of course," I replied. I know she expected a different answer.

Just before they signed off, we heard a bang. Jim Lovell said, "Houston, that bang you heard was Fred Haise on the cabin repress valve. He really gets our hearts going with that one every time." Fred liked to kid around.

"Our next broadcast will be from Fra Mauro on the surface of the Moon," Jim said. Fra Mauro was a region of hills. The scientists had chosen the area for a landing because they thought the hills had been created by volcanoes. Moon scientists get all excited about volcanoes.

I got up and stretched. "Thanks, Mom, for letting me come," I said.

"We better get ready to go home," she said.

"Okay," I said. "But I want to thank Mr. Kranz first."

I walked out of the room. Then I heard one of the controllers say, "Give the oxygen tanks a stir."

In a few minutes, Jack Swigert said, "Are you copying O2 tank one pressure?"

"That's affirmative," said someone at Mission Control. The tank was losing oxygen.

Another man stood up and said to Gene Kranz, "I want to shut off the reactant valves, starting with fuel cell three first, to see if we can stop the flows." Once the valves shut down, they couldn't be reopened. That meant *Apollo 13* couldn't complete its mission.

You could feel the disappointment in the room. On the spacecraft, when they were told to shut the valves, Fred Haise said, "Did I hear you right? You want me to shut the reac valve on fuel cell three?"

"That's affirmative," came the reply.

"It's over," Jim Lovell said with a sigh. "We're not going to the Moon."

Then came the news that shutting down the valve didn't stop the oxygen from leaking into space. They shut down fuel tank number one, but got the same result.

How would the astronauts be able to breathe? I wondered. The men of Mission Control thought of putting the crew into the lunar module. It had its own oxygen supplies.

"That's what we're thinking too," Jim replied.

Are they going to die? I wondered. These were my friends. I lost my father, now I was going to lose these men, too.

"Ramón?" I felt my mother's touch. "It's very late. We must leave," she said.

"But, Mom, what about Mr. Lovell and the crew?"

"There is nothing more we can do," she said.

CHAPTER 3

CLOSE TO DISASTER

When we arrived home, I ran to my room and turned on the squawk box. I'm sure my mother knew I was listening, but she left me alone.

At Mission Control, Mr. Kranz's team was turning control over to Glynn Lunney's team of controllers. I heard Lunney say, "Get them into the LM! We've got to get oxygen on!"

"Houston," Jim Lovell called. "I've got some numbers for you, but I want you to double-check my arithmetic so far."

Jim told me he had trouble with math. The math had to be just right, or they were finished. This time, adding up the numbers meant life or death.

Jim called out the numbers, and then there was silence. I'm sure the men inside *Apollo 13* were holding their breaths, hearts pounding. Then, Lousma came on. "Okay, *Aquarius*, your arithmetic looks good."

"Okay," Jim said after a while. "*Aquarius* is up and *Odyssey* is completely powered down."

"Roger," Lousma replied.

I heard Jim say, "Is there any way I can control this thing? I want to get out of this roll."

"It doesn't matter where you go," Mission Control replied.

"Are we still leaking oxygen?" Jim asked.

"We're not," they said.

I sat on the edge of my bed. Jim Lovell was a great pilot. But if he couldn't get the ship under control, they wouldn't be able to get home.

I went back to my room and lay on my bed. Then I heard Jack Lousma's voice over the squawk box. "*Aquarius*, we'd like to brief you on what our burn plan is." He explained that they would fire engines on *Aquarius* to slingshot the spacecraft around the Moon and send it to Earth.

A little later, Fred said, "So long Earth, catch you on the flipside." And *Apollo 13* disappeared around the dark side of the Moon.

• • •

Many of the kids at school had parents who worked at the Johnson Space Center, so the TVs were on in the classrooms.

We waited and watched, hoping *Apollo 13* would circle the Moon and head home for Earth. Fred Haise had told me that the rockets on *Aquarius* were for lunar landing or take off. They weren't designed to steer the whole spacecraft.

"*Apollo 13* has rounded the Moon, and is on a trajectory for Earth," we heard the TV report.

We cheered. Still, everyone worried. Except, of course, for Terry Urban.

Mr. Morales calmed the class. "Ramón, what do you think?"

A few months ago, I would have met Terry after school and gotten into a fight. "If Terry could see the activity and worry at Mission Control, he would know that this isn't a hoax," I nearly shouted. "I've seen the controllers and the others working night and day to bring those men back."

"Yeah? Well, I'd like to see that myself to believe it," said Terry.

"Then maybe you should," I said. "Come with me, and I'll prove it!"

Mr. Morales smiled.

"Okay," Terry said. "But I'll bet those buildings are fake too."

CHAPTER 4

LESSONS LEARNED

After school, Terry and I boarded the bus for the space center.

"My folks were so mad at me for fighting that they grounded me for months," said Terry. "I guess when Mr. Morales told them that this would be a good learning experience, they agreed to let me come with you."

"It will be worth it," I said.

"But I really came because I want to see for myself how fake the whole thing is," he said.

When we entered the center, Terry's eyes grew wide. I knew he might be rethinking his ideas. Then Gene Kranz spotted me. I took Terry over to meet him.

Nice to meet you, Terry. Are you here to help?

Yes, s-s-sir.

You have a good friend in Ramón. He's part of the team trying to bring our astronauts home.

Wow!

Come on, Terry, we have to bring meals to the guys in the simulators.

My cousin said the whole thing was filmed in the simulators.

Ha! Just wait!

We entered building five and brought the food to men working on the simulators.

"We did it," I heard John Aaron say. "By running the battery from the LM to the CM, we can give them enough power."

You could feel the excitement in the room. Even Terry smiled.

Terry and I caught a ride back to Mission Control, and we went to the VIP room. I could see how excited Terry had become. "This is cool."

The control room suddenly grew quiet. Time for a mid-course burn. To fire the LM's engine, Jim had to line up on the Earth to navigate.

"Jack," Jim told Swigert. "You time the burn with your watch. We're firing for 14 seconds."

"Fred, you grab the attitude controller," said Lovell. "I'll handle pitch and roll and take care of ignition and shutdown."

Five, four, three, two, one.

Ignition!

Roger. Shutdown. Good burn, *Aquarius.*

Shutdown! Houston, burn complete.

They're really up there, aren't they?

They sure are.

The next day, Thursday, April 16, was very tense. At school, we learned Fred Haise was running a fever. He and the rest of the crew hadn't been drinking enough water.

After school, Terry and I returned to the Space Center to learn some more bad news. We listened as the CapCom called *Apollo*. "You're coming in on a slightly shallow flight path," he said.

"What does that mean?" Terry asked.

"It means they might hit the atmosphere and bounce back into space," I answered.

"Can't they try again?" he asked.

"No," I replied. "They only have one chance."

Terry stayed at my place that night. I turned on the squawk box. Ken Mattingly was reading instructions to the crew.

School closed on Friday. The world was watching. Terry and I watched at Mission Control.

You could feel the tension. Terry and I kept very quiet as we passed out coffee. Gene Kranz was in charge once again. Jim fired the jets on *Aquarius* for a last course correction. Now it was time to separate the damaged service module.

"When you jettison the service module, Jim and Fred, stay in the LM," said Mission Control. "Jack, go to the CM. Just before you separate, Jim will fire the LM thrusters, pushing the craft forward. Jack will cut the service module."

"When do you want us to do this?" Fred asked.

"Time is not critical," Mission Control replied.

The astronauts went to their stations. I was so nervous, I spilled Mr. Kranz's coffee on my shirt.

Then Jim called, "Jack, you ready?"

"All set," said Mission Control.

"When you feel the motion, let 'er go," the controller added. "Five, four, three, two, one!"

Jack sang out, "Jettison!"

"Maneuver complete," said Mission Control.

I looked at Terry, and he smiled with relief. Now it was time to power up the *Odyssey*.

"If those electric panels are wet from the cold air, when Jack throws those switches," I whispered to Terry, "they'll start a fire."

As Jack fired up the CM, we held our breath.

"Okay, Houston," Jim called. "I'm at the LM separation attitude, ready to bail out."

Once the men were all in *Odyssey*, Jack flipped a switch, and he called, "LM jettison complete."

"Now, they only have that little capsule to get them back to Earth," I said.

Gene Kranz ran a check of all the controller stations. Each controller answered with a "go."

CapCom relayed the message. "We'll have a loss of signal in about a minute." The speed of the reentry would cause the astronaut's to black out for a few minutes.

We waited to hear from *Odyssey*. "What if the heat shield fails?" I wondered under my breath. They'd burn up. We'd know in three minutes. No crew had ever taken longer than three minutes to emerge from a blackout. -

Three minutes dragged slowly by, and we heard nothing. Then four minutes. I bit my lip to stop myself from yelling. Terry was squeezing his eyes shut tight, but I could see his tears.

"*Odyssey*, Houston standing by, over."

Fifteen seconds passed.

"Houston standing by, over."

Thirty seconds.

Nothing but static.

In the end, the crew was safe. Soon, they were picked up by helicopter and taken to the deck of a carrier ship. It was great watching Jim Lovell, Fred Haise, and Jack Swigert step onto the deck of that ship.

Later, investigators discovered that the oxygen tank had been faulty, and the men could not have prevented the accident. Some say *Apollo* 13 was a disaster. I say it was a triumph of science, engineering, and hard work, along with bravery, that brought the crew home.

As for me, I studied hard, graduated from the Naval Academy, became a Marine flyer, and eventually joined NASA. I flew a number of space shuttle missions. Terry Urban became a flight surgeon and flew on shuttle missions, too.

We still joke about how we fought.

Gary Bush writes full time for both the children and adult markets. He is currently doing research for a young adult novel about Barbary Pirates. Bush is the co-editor of the forthcoming anthology, *Once upon a Crime*, stories from some of the world's top mystery authors. He lives in Minneapolis, Minnesota, with his wife, Stacey, and their Kerry blue terrier, Homer.

Glossary

emerge (i-MURJ)—to come out of concealment

hoax (HOHKS)—fake, or a trick

miracle (MIHR-uh-kuhl)—an amazing and unlikely event

routine (ROO-teen)—normal and not difficult or unusual at all

simulator (SIM-yuh-lay-tur)—a machine that allows you to experience what it is like to pilot a spaceship

technicians (teck-NISH-uhns)—people who work with specialized equipment

trajectory (truh-JEK-tuh-ree)—the curved path that a rocket or ship travels in flight

triumph (TRYE-uhmf)—a great victory or success

The space mission *Apollo 13* began on April 11, 1970. The spacecraft, with three astronauts onboard, launched without problems. Two days after the launch, one of two oxygen tanks onboard the ship exploded at a distance of almost 330,000 kilometers from Earth. The explosion damaged the spacecraft and caused a loss of oxygen and electricity. The mission to reach the Moon was now impossible to complete. But the mission is known as "A Successful Failure" because many difficult problems were overcome to bring the astronauts home safely.

Mission Control, along with the crew on the spacecraft, brainstormed together to try to figure out a way to get the crew home. However, the second oxygen tank was also damaged in the explosion. The spacecraft relied on the oxygen tanks to generate electricity, so the damage to the oxygen tanks meant that limited power was available for the spacecraft. The batteries onboard could only last for ten hours, and they needed to be saved for reentering Earth's atmosphere during landing, so the crew survived by using the lunar module as a lifeboat.

Eventually, they decided that they would use the Moon's gravity to "slingshot" the spacecraft back to Earth! They activated the ship's power to catapult it into the gravitational pull of the Moon, which sent them soaring back toward Earth.

The astronauts onboard may have been saved by another failure in the oxygen tanks. Two days into the mission, the second oxygen tank wasn't functioning properly. The crew had to stir the tanks earlier than originally planned, which caused the tank to explode. If the error hadn't occurred, they would have waited until after landing on the Moon to stir the tank, which would have delayed the explosion. It's likely that the crew would not have made it home safely because there would have been less of the spacecraft's supplies and power left.

The *Apollo 13* astronauts and the Mission Control team were awarded the Presidential Medal of Freedom for their actions and quick thinking during the mission. *Apollo 14* completed *Apollo 13's* mission successfully on February 5, 1971.

1. Think about Ramón's experience working at Johnson Space Center. What sort of impact did it make on his life?

2. The crew of *Apollo 13* became important influences in Ramón's life. What qualities did they possess that helped and inspired Ramón?

3. The story of *Apollo 13* has been the subject of several books and movies. Why do you think this story has been so popular?

1. Astronaut Ken Mattingly was disappointed to
   learn that he couldn't go on the mission since
   he was exposed to measles. Write about a time
   when you were disappointed. How did you
   feel? Did someone try to make you feel better?

2. Ramón set the goal of becoming an astronaut.
   What do you hope to become when you grow
   up? What classes and skills are important to
   reach your goal?

3. Ramón and Terry start out the book as
   enemies. After getting to know each other
   better, they become friends. Have you ever had
   a similar experience? Write about it.

Internet Sites

Do you want to know more about subjects related to this book? Or are you interested in learning about other topics? Then check out FactHound, a fun, easy way to find Internet sites.

Our investigative staff has already sniffed out great sites for you!

Here's how to use FactHound:

1. Visit *www.facthound.com*

2. Select your grade level.

3. To learn more about subjects related to this book, type in the book's ISBN number: 9781434211620.

4. Click the Fetch It button.

FactHound will fetch the best Internet sites for you.